Hello Kitty's Family Trip

By Kris Hirschmann
Illustrated by Sachiho Hino

ISBN-13: 978-0-545-06115-5
ISBN-10: 0-545-06115-6

12 11 10 9 8 7 6 5 4 3 2 1   9 10 11 12 13 14/0
Printed in the U.S.A.
First printing, March 2009

SCHOLASTIC INC.
New York Toronto London Auckland Sydney
Mexico City New Delhi Hong Kong Buenos Aires

 and sat in the lunchroom

at . The friends were talking

about spring break.

"My family is going to the ,"

said . "What are you doing?"

"We're going camping," said .

"Can you visit me at the ?"

asked.

"I don't think so," said . "We'll

be too far away."

"I'll miss you," said .

 hugged her friend. "I'll write you lots of . I'll give you all of the  when  starts again."

"Me, too," said . "I'll think about you every day, !"

 packed for her trip. She filled

half of her with . She filled

the other half with and .

looked at her full . "I'm

going to be writing a lot of !"

 and her family drove to the campground the next morning. wanted to write to during the drive. But then she saw a covered with tiny green .

"Look! Spring !" she said to her sister, .

 spent the rest of the drive looking out her .

8

 set up her . Then she got

out her and .

"Now I can write to 🐑," she said.

🐱 heard a sound outside her 🏕 .

It was a family of 🐥 . Seven baby

🐥 waddled behind their mother.

"Oh, how sweet!" cried 🐱 . She

leaped up and followed the 🐥 .

🐱 forgot all about writing .

 woke up early the next

morning.

"I'll write to 🐑 today," she said.

But she didn't have time. 🐱 and

🐱 took 🐱 and 🐱 on a 🧺

in a grassy ▬ .

🐱 ate, played with 🐱, and

enjoyed the spring ☀ on her face.

 glanced at her and

the next day. She should write to

.

"But it's such a nice day," she said to

. "Let's go pick ."

They ran to a nearby .

and picked all day

long.

They had a great time.

 didn't write any  the next day. She was busy catching  in the .

"There are so many fun things to do in the spring!" she said as she put the  into a .

The days flew by. Soon it was time to

pack up and go home.

 picked up her . She opened

her . There she saw all of her

unused .

"Oh, no! I didn't write to !" cried

. She felt terrible.

 was afraid to see  at

the next day.

Would be upset?

 walked over to her friend.

"I'm so, so sorry, . I had a fun

time at the . But I forgot to write

you any ," said. "Are you

mad at me?"

"Of course I'm not mad. You're my best friend," said . "Besides . . . I forgot to write, too."

"I guess we both had fun," said with a smile.

 smiled. "I have a feeling we both had the best spring break ever!"

Did you spot all the picture clues in this Hello Kitty book?

Each picture clue is on a flash card. Ask a grown-up to cut out the flash cards. Then try reading the words on the backs of the cards. The pictures will be your clue.

Reading is fun with Hello Kitty!

beach	Hello Kitty
letters	Fifi
bag	school

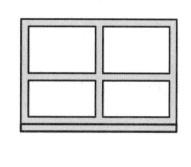

Mama	window
Papa	tent
picnic	ducks

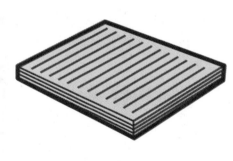

tree	clothes
leaves	paper
Mimmy	pencils

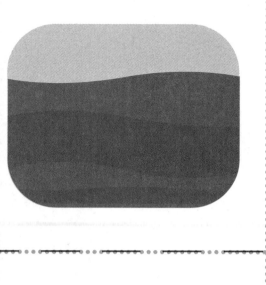

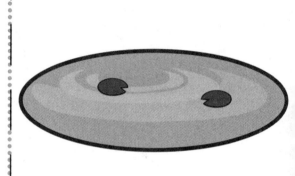

frogs	meadow
pond	sun
pail	flowers